DK READERS

1 TO READ

Truck Trouble

BE-16-88

Written by Angela Royston

DK

A Dorling Kindersley Book

John got up very early
to make a special delivery.
He climbed up two steps
into his big blue truck.

John looked at the map.
He had no time to get lost!
Then he started the truck,
checked the mirrors and set off.

mirror

At the service station,
John checked the engine.
It needed some oil.
Then he filled up the fuel tank.

fuel tank

He looked at
the shiny engine.
"Don't let me down!"
he said.
"I can't be late!"

Next he had to pick up his load.
A fork-lift truck lifted big boxes
into the back of John's truck.

There were also some small boxes
marked "Special Delivery".
John put these in the truck too.

John was in a hurry
but he was also
very hungry.

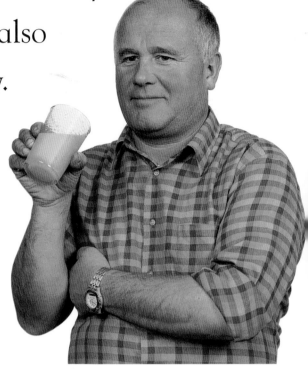

He pulled into a rest area
for breakfast.

John's friend Paul arrived
in his milk tanker.
He joined John for breakfast.

John couldn't stop for long.
He had two deliveries to make.

John drove onto the motorway.

It was jammed with traffic.

Cars and trucks beeped their horns.

John had to deliver the big boxes
to a nearby factory.
He left the motorway
at the next exit.

John waved to the workers as
he drove into the factory.

The workers helped him
to unload the big boxes.

"I'm in a hurry,"
John told them.
"I've got another delivery
to make."
He was soon on his way.
But there was trouble ahead!

A van had broken down!
John slammed on the brakes and
his truck screeched to a halt.

The road was very narrow.
John's truck was too wide
to get past the van.

John used his radio to call for help.
He also warned other drivers
to stay away from that road.

Soon John saw flashing lights.
It was a tow truck!
The tow truck towed the van
to a garage.

When the road was clear
John hurried on his way.
But there was more trouble ahead!

Boom! Boom!

John drove into a thunderstorm.

Rain began to pour down.

John turned on
the windscreen wipers.

wiper

He drove very slowly.

"This isn't my day!"

he groaned.

John drove on and on.
At last the rain stopped and
he pulled over to eat his lunch.

Then he rested on a bunk
in the back of the cab.
He fell fast asleep!

When he woke up, John thought,
"Now I'm in trouble!"

John drove off. BANG!
"Oh no! A flat tyre!"
He grabbed
his tools and
the spare wheel.

John unscrewed
the bolts and
took off the wheel.

bolt

Then he put on the spare wheel.
It was very hard work!

John drove into town.
He had to wait for
a set of traffic lights
to turn green.

traffic
lights

BE-16-88

"Hurry up!" thought John.
It was time to make
his special delivery.

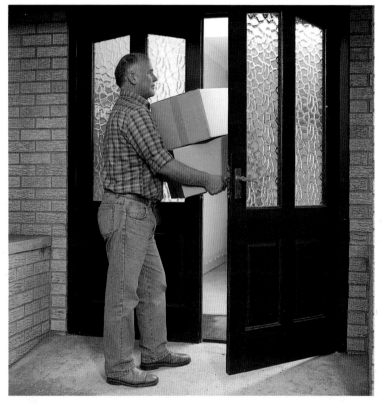

John arrived at last.
There was no time to spare!
He unloaded the boxes marked
"Special Delivery".

John was just in time for the party at the new children's hospital.

Inside the special boxes
were piles of toys.
"Thank you!" shouted the children.
"It was no trouble!" said John.

Glossary

Bolt
a screw without a point used to fasten things

Fuel tank
a large container for storing fuel

Mirror
a piece of glass that helps you to see what's behind you

Traffic lights
a row of red, yellow and green lights that control traffic

Wiper
a long thin tool that wipes away water